The letter said that Miss Pink Cat gave her permission for someone else to collect the necklace.

Little did Miss Pink Cat and Noddy realise that two goblins were hiding close by, listening to them.

"Sly, we shall have that necklace!" Gobbo chuckled mischievously.

Sniggering at how cunning they were, the goblins crept up to Clockwork Mouse.

"Would you like to earn sixpence?" Gobbo asked him. "All you have to do is find Noddy and tell him that Miss Pink Cat has decided to collect the gold necklace herself!"

Noddy and the Goblins

Collins
An Imprint of HarperCollins*Publishers*

MARTH

MR PLOD

MASTER TUBBY BEAR

ONKEY

SLY

MR WOBBLY MAN

BUMPY DOG

It was a busy morning in Toyland . . .

Miss Pink Cat had a very important job for Noddy.

"I want you to go to the station to meet the train and fetch a parcel sent by my Great Aunt, containing a most valuable gold necklace!" she told him grandly.

She gave Noddy a letter to show to Mr Train Driver.

Clockwork Mouse found Noddy outside his house.

Noddy thought it rather strange when Clockwork Mouse told him that Miss Pink Cat had decided to collect the necklace herself. But he just shrugged his shoulders and handed over the letter Miss Pink Cat had given him so Clockwork Mouse could return it to her.

Clockwork Mouse took Miss Pink Cat's letter to the goblins. They immediately took it to the station.

"Hello, Mr Train Driver," said Gobbo.

"Miss Pink Cat's sent us for a parcel," Sly told Mr Train Driver. "Read this letter."

Mr Train Driver was not sure whether he should trust the goblins. They were always playing such naughty tricks.

But there was no doubt that Gobbo had Miss Pink Cat's letter. So Mr Train Driver handed them the parcel containing the gold necklace.

Of course, Miss Pink Cat did not know about any of the goblins' mischievous doings. She still thought Noddy had gone to the station for her.

"Noddy! Have you been to the station?" she demanded when she met him.

Noddy tried to explain to Miss Pink Cat about Clockwork Mouse's message but of course she did not know what he was talking about. She just threatened to report Noddy to Mr Plod! Noddy became very upset.

"I must find Clockwork Mouse," he decided glumly.

"So there you are, Clockwork Mouse!" Noddy declared sternly when he found him at Market Square. "Did you take Miss Pink Cat's parcel?"

Clockwork Mouse looked quite scared. “No, I didn’t, Noddy!” he answered quickly. “It’s the goblins who are to blame. They said I could have sixpence if...”

But Noddy had already marched off in search of the goblins!

Noddy found the goblins at the café. Creeping up on them, he saw that Miss Pink Cat's special parcel was there as well!

"I thought as much!" Noddy gasped.

Noddy ran off to the police station so he could explain everything to Mr Plod.

“It’s Sly and Gobbo, Mr Plod! They’ve been tricking everybody! They tricked Clockwork Mouse into taking Miss Pink Cat’s letter! And they tricked Mr Train Driver into giving them her parcel containing...” Noddy ran out of breath.

"...containing a most valuable gold necklace," concluded Mr Plod who had just talked to Miss Pink Cat.

Mr Plod asked Noddy to follow him to the café. He wanted to talk to those two goblins!

"Now then, Sly and Gobbo!" Mr Plod barked as soon as he and Noddy had reached the café. "I have some questions to ask you!"

The goblins did not want to answer any questions, however. They immediately leapt up from their table and ran off!

“Wait! I want to speak you!” Mr Plod bellowed as he and Noddy started to chase after the goblins.

Noddy and Mr Plod ran very fast. They started to close in on the goblins but Sly and Gobbo were not beaten yet.

The goblins leapt into Mr Sparks' car and drove it away at full speed!

“I’ll catch them in my car, Mr Plod!” Noddy shouted.
Noddy drove off at full speed as well, his tyres squealing for all they were worth.

“Look at that fast car!” the Skittle children cried excitedly as Noddy sped past them.

The Skittles were so excited that they all tumbled over.

“This is such an exciting day!” they said, giggling with delight.

“Faster, Gobbo!” Sly cried as the two cars sped through the countryside. “Noddy’s catching us up!”

Noddy drove faster than he had ever driven before.

"I'm sorry for driving so fast, little car," he said anxiously. "Please don't crash!"

But it was the goblins' car that crashed!

"Help! Where's the brakes?" Gobbo yelled as he suddenly lost control of the steering wheel and their car swerved about wildly.

The goblins' car crashed straight into a rock!

"My poor arm!" cried Gobbo.

"My poor nose!" squealed Sly.

Something had flown out of the goblins' car when they crashed. It was Miss Pink Cat's package! It landed neatly in Big-Ears' hands.

"Oh, Big-Ears – you are clever!" Noddy cried.

"You've found Miss Pink Cat's gold necklace!" Noddy explained to Big-Ears. "The goblins took it!"

Big-Ears marched towards the goblins.

"Then we must take them to see Mr Plod!" he declared with a stern scowl at them both.

Noddy took the package containing the gold necklace to Miss Pink Cat.

To begin with, she was quite cross with Noddy, thinking it was *he* who had tried to steal her necklace. She thought this was why it had taken Noddy so long to deliver the package.

But then Big-Ears explained to Miss Pink Cat that it was the goblins who stole her necklace.

"Noddy chased them in his car all alone!" he added proudly. "He was very brave!"

Miss Pink Cat broke into a big grateful smile.

"Ah, but of course! Noddy shall have a reward. Do you like eggs for your tea?" she asked.

"Oh yes!" cried Noddy.

"Then you shall have enough sixpences to buy the six finest eggs in Toy Town!" chuckled Miss Pink Cat.

This edition first published in Great Britain by HarperCollins Publishers Ltd in 2000

1 3 5 7 9 10 8 6 4 2

For further information on Enid Blyton please contact www.blyton.com

ISBN: 0 00 136174 0

A CIP catalogue for this title is available from the British Library.

The HarperCollins website address is:
www.**fire**and**water**.com

Reproduction by Graphic Studio S.r.l. Verona
Printed in Italy by Garzanti Verga S.r.l.

MORE NODDY BOOKS FOR YOU TO ENJOY

Noddy and the Artists

Noddy and the Bouncing Ball

Noddy and the Noisy Drum

Noddy Tidies Toyland

Noddy and the Singing Bush

Noddy and the Treasure Map

Noddy is Caught in a Storm

Noddy and the Driving Lesson

Noddy is Far Too Busy

Noddy and the Magic Watch

Noddy the Nurse

Noddy Tells a Story